The Emperor's New Clothes

Written by Hans Christian Andersen

Retold by Susie Day

Illustrated by Monica Auriemma

Collins

Chapter 1

The Emperor of Sarn was a very proud man. His empire stretched 5,000 kilometres in every direction, from snow-topped mountains in the north to the golden beaches of the southern coast, from dunes in the east to the deep western forests.

He lived in a fine palace in the city of Blotch, with his wife Ingrid, his soldiers, and many servants.

The emperor didn't care if his people were happy. He wasn't interested in fighting wars. He never read his advisers' reports on the failing wheat harvest, or the rising tides. He didn't even care for his beautiful palace. All he cared about were clothes.

His wardrobes were so stuffed, the doors wouldn't shut.
He had cloaks of fur and velvet, in every shade of blue and
green and pink and purple. He had waistcoats embroidered
with pictures of his own face. His underwear alone took up
half a room: spotty woolly vests and stripy long johns –
in matching colours, of course.

Every New Year, the emperor walked through the city of Blotch at the head of a grand parade.

"But I've nothing at all to wear!" he whined one year. (Emperors always have whiny voices.) "Ingrid! This is an emergency! Bring me a dressmaker at once – I must have new clothes!"

Chapter 2

Far from the palace lived two dressmaker sisters: bold
Asta and careful Anita. Asta wove cloth on her loom, with
fingers that flew. Anita neatly cut, and sewed and stitched.
But they were so poor, they often had no wool to weave
into cloth, or thread to stitch it, and when the coal for
the fire ran out, their hands were too stiff to work.

"If only it could be us," sighed Anita, when she heard the emperor wanted a new dressmaker. "But he'll expect silk, or furs. We could never – "

But Asta smiled slyly. "Oh, sister! I've an idea. And the emperor – he'll never see it coming!"

7

Every dressmaker in Blotch came to the palace – but not one outfit was good enough for the emperor.

"Too orange!"

"Too flouncy!"

"Too short! I fear my ankles will be chilly
– don't you think so, Sir Boris?"

8

Sir Boris was the emperor's favourite adviser, for he always said whatever the emperor most wanted to hear.

"Quite so, your imperial majesty," he said, bowing. "I shall have the dressmakers locked up at once for chilling your ankles!"

The emperor slumped on his golden throne. "Is there no one else?"

"Two sisters, sir," said Sir Boris doubtfully, "from the market district."

The emperor sighed. "Bring them in," he said.

Anita gasped as they were led into the fine throne room. The emperor himself was there!

Asta strode forwards boldly. "Observe, sir, the beautiful cloth we've made for you. The turquoise threads ... this bronze embroidery – "

She held out her arms. They were quite empty. "Oh!" she said, with a twinkle in her eye. "I forgot to say – our cloth is very special. It's invisible to anyone stupid, or unworthy."

Anita trembled, certain they'd be thrown out, or worse. But no one wanted to seem stupid or unworthy – least of all the emperor.

"I love it!" he squeaked.
"You will make my new clothes!"

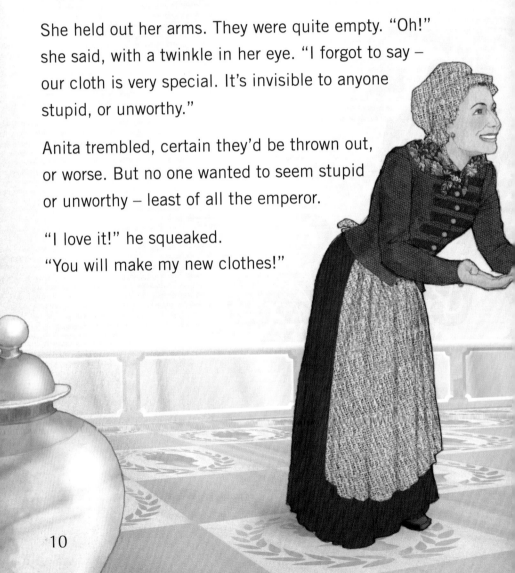

Chapter 3

The emperor gave the sisters three bags of gold as payment for his new clothes. It was more money than Anita had ever seen! They spent it on food, and enough coal to keep the fire burning all winter.

Three days later, back in the palace, the emperor began to worry. "Sir Boris! Go to those dressmakers, and check on my new clothes."

Sir Boris knocked hard on the sisters' door.

Anita grew frightened.

But Asta was as bold as ever. "Come in, sir! As you can see, the robes are coming along splendidly! See the pearl buttons … the silvery thread here, like spider's webs – "

Of course, there was nothing to see but an empty wooden coat hanger.

But Sir Boris was so afraid of looking stupid that he smiled, and nodded, as if he could see robes decorated like spider's webs, with pearl buttons. "Ladies, your skill is remarkable!" he said, bowing deeply. "I'll report back to the emperor at once, and assure him all's well with his new clothes!"

After he was gone, Anita clapped her hands with joy.
"Oh Asta, I think your plan is working!"

She made hot chocolate for everyone in their cold,
dark street, even little Krister, the street boy. She gave
him the largest cup.

Chapter 4

It was only three days till New Year. The emperor was still worried.

"Ingrid! Go to those dressmakers, and check on my robes!"

The sisters showed her the same empty wooden coat hanger – but the emperor's wife was so afraid of looking unworthy, she smiled as if she saw magnificent robes.

"I'd love to add a hat, of blue velvet," said Asta slyly, "but alas, we've run out of gold."

Ingrid dashed back to the palace. Hours later, another bag of gold arrived. The sisters bought enough food for a feast for the whole street: stew, and hot potatoes and chicken legs.

Chapter 5

New Year came, and a blanket of snow covered
the city of Blotch.

The emperor wore his second-favourite clothes for
the palace feast: a purple furry jacket and yellow trousers.
"These aren't my new clothes," he said, loudly. "I'll have
new clothes for the parade."

The sisters were collected by carriage – they'd never ridden in one before and Anita found it so exciting – and brought directly to the emperor's own dressing room.

Anita's hands wouldn't stop trembling as she held the empty wooden coat hanger. "Surely he'll realise," she whispered, "now the parade's here?"

But Asta shook her head. "Trust me!" she said.

The emperor skipped into the dressing room – wearing nothing but his underwear – clapping his hands with excitement.

Asta pretended to drape robes over his shoulders. Anita pretended to do up the pearly buttons.

"It feels very ... light," said the emperor, frowning as he turned this way and that before the mirror. All he could see was his underwear!

"Magical cloth always feels light, sir," promised
Anita, nervously. "Like spider's webs."

The emperor remembered what the sisters had said:
the cloth was only invisible to the stupid or unworthy.
He couldn't admit to that!

Asta bowed. "Your majesty, your people will see a whole
new side of you."

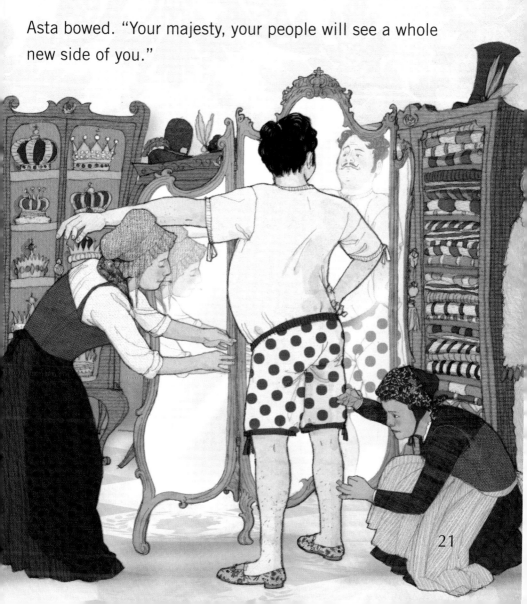

Chapter 6

The emperor strode through the palace in his underwear, his chest puffed out with pride.

"Don't I look magnificent?" he asked, twirling before Ingrid, who was dressed in purple velvet.

"Isn't this hat simply remarkable?" he asked Sir Boris, who wore golden furs.

"Have you ever seen new clothes like these in your life?" he asked his soldiers, standing ready at the palace gate.

All they could see was his underwear! But not one of them dared to admit it.

Bells rang out across Blotch, to signal the start of the New Year parade.

"At last!" said the emperor. "This parade will be the best yet!"

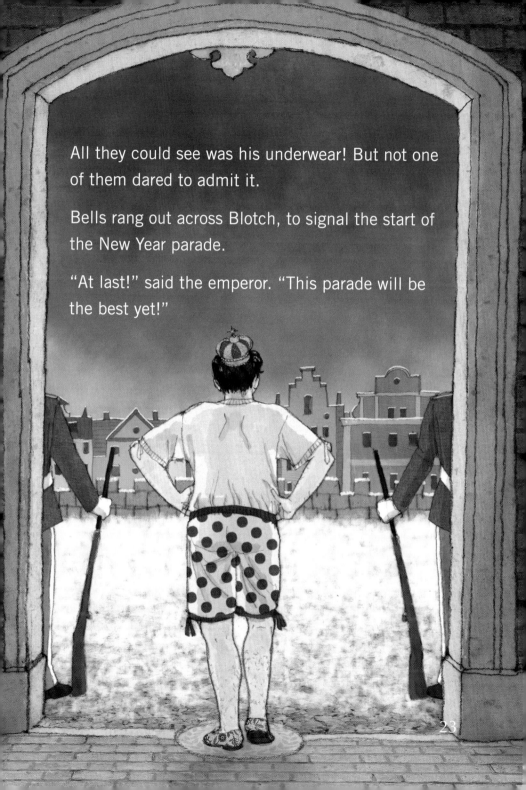

Blotch was busy with parade music and bright flags.
The streets were lined with people, all wrapped
up warm against the winter air.

"Hello, my people! It's me, your beloved emperor!"
he called, waving.

Everywhere he walked, there were gasps from the crowd.

"I know, I look amazing!" he cried, twirling so that
everyone could see his new clothes.

All they could see was his underwear! But not one dared to say a word.

A light snow began to fall. The emperor felt very cold indeed – as if he was wearing almost nothing at all. *It's magical cloth*, he reminded himself, *like spider's webs*.

The parade entered the dull, crooked streets of
the market district.

Krister, the little street boy, pushed to the front.
"That man's got no clothes on!" he shouted, pointing
his finger straight at the emperor.

The emperor froze.

The crowd began to whisper, then giggle, then
laugh out loud. "He's right! It's true! He's got no
clothes on, ha ha ha!"

The emperor looked down, and saw what they all could see: his underwear, on display for all.

"Eek! Guards! Help!"

But his soldiers were laughing too.

The emperor wrapped himself in a stripy blanket from a nearby market stall, and ran away, yelping at the cold.

The laughter rippled through Blotch all night long.

In the market district, there was dancing and music, a bonfire to warm the hands, and food and drink for all, bought with the emperor's gold.

"I still can't believe it worked!" whispered Anita.

"Me neither," said Asta, laughing.

That night, the sisters went back to their cosy little home, and slept soundly.

And the emperor? He was never seen again.

But if you visit the city of Blotch at New Year, you'll hear the laughter as someone walks the parade, dressed in the emperor's new clothes.

SISTERLY

ARE YOU READY FOR A NEW LOOK?

COME TO ASTA AND ANITA

DESIGNS

for the best new clothes

ONE OF A KIND

IN EVERY COLOUR YOU CAN IMAGINE

ONE SIZE FITS ALL

So lightweight you won't know you're wearing a stitch!

Ideas for reading

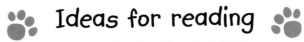

Written by Clare Dowdall, PhD
Lecturer and Primary Literacy Consultant

Reading objectives:
- increase familiarity with a wide range of books including fairy stories and retell orally
- identify themes and conventions in a wide range of books
- make predictions from details stated and applied
- identify main ideas drawn from more than one paragraph and summarise ideas

Spoken language objectives:
- give well-structured descriptions, explanations and narratives for different purposes
- participate in discussions, presentations, performances, role play, improvisations and debates

Curriculum links: PSHE – self management; design technology

Resources: paper and pens

Build a context for reading

- Ask children what they'd wear if they could have an outfit designed for a special party.
- Look at the emperor on the front cover. Ask for adjectives and similes to describe him.
- Ask children to read the blurb to themselves, then share their predictions about what Asta and Anita might plan to do.

Understand and apply reading strategies

- Read Chapter 1 aloud to the children. Ask them to listen for information about the emperor's character.
- Model reading aloud with storytelling expression, using a whining voice for the emperor.
- Ask children to give examples of the emperor's selfishness, and back up their ideas with evidence from the story, e.g. he had his face embroidered on his waistcoats.
- Ask children to continue reading to see what happens.